THE SHADOW

MATTHEW THORNTON

DEDICATION

[to be sent by client]

ACKNOWLEDGMENT

The three main people I'd like to acknowledge are Henery Parker, Shea Cater, and Kim Anderson. Henery Parker and Shea Cater supported me throughout the entire journey of my writing, and Kim Anderson helped inspire me to finish and publish it.

CONTENTS

ABOUT THE AUTHOR

[to be sent by client]

CHAPTER 1

It was a bright sunny day when Sebastian arrived in that sleepy little town of Pretton, Missouri. Pretton was mostly made up of farmers and the town at first glance held very little to admire.

The town itself had one gas station, a small grocery store, a feed store, and a few other essentials needed to keep the farmers in business around the area.

He drove past the first row of battered buildings and felt the street's quiet press in around him. So quiet he found himself glancing in the mirrors more than once. A few townspeople threw him quick, wary looks, the kind that slipped away the instant you caught their eyes.

Sebastian had decided to move to Pretton from Houston in an effort to change his surroundings since he no longer had any reason to stay in Houston after being discharged from the Marines.

The fresh start sounded good in theory, but even as he rolled through Pretton for the first time, he felt that faint prickle down the back of his neck that told him this place was not going to be as simple as it looked.

So, with his truck and a small trailer, he packed his stuff and moved. Most of what he owned fit into a few boxes, and the old furniture he had held onto through every duty station, the kind of things you carry more out of habit than attachment. He had found a small three-bedroom farmhouse that he bought with a loan that he got for having served his country. The place wasn't much, but the quiet road leading to it and the open fields around it gave him the sense that maybe he could breathe here for the first time in a while.

With him being awarded the Purple Heart and a silver star for his efforts in a skirmish with the Taliban on a routine patrol had helped him with the loan by being exempted from the funding fees associated with the loans. Sebastian did not think about the medals too often, he mostly tried not to but every now and then the memory of that day crept in, sharp and unwelcome, reminding him what it had cost to earn them.

Sebastian started reflecting on the day he earned his medals; he was always credited as the calm in every storm. Always known for not spooking easily during any sign of trouble, he was the sole survivor keeping the insurgents at bay with his rifle while everyone around him began falling to the RPG and small arms fire. Sebastian had taken a 7.62×54R round from an SVD-style sniper rifle, the kind commonly carried by Taliban marksmen, through the shoulder, yet he kept fighting, earning him the Purple Heart and the Silver Star.

Even now, it came back in pieces. Dust in the air. Ringing in his ears. Someone is shouting his name. Sometimes a sound or a smell would hit him out of nowhere, and he'd see it all again before he could blink. He never thought he'd done anything heroic. He just wanted everyone to get home. His shoulder still hurt when it got cold. Some nights it woke him up. A reminder. Of how close he'd come to not walking away.

Shaking his head clear, Sebastian started unpacking his stuff when he noticed a weird stain on the floor. It was not big, but it stood out against the rest of the boards, darker and sunk a little deeper into the grain, like whatever caused it had been there a long time. He crouched for a second, trying to make sense of it, but the house was quiet and empty and he figured he was overthinking it.

Thinking nothing of it, he decided to cover it up with his couch he had brought with him. It took about four hours for him to unpack his stuff and by the time he was finished he felt satisfied with how everything looked. He had set his couch at a perfect spot so that it aligned with his recliner that he had set at a forty-five degree offset to his TV with its two perfectly symmetrical speakers. Lining things up calmed him down more than he cared to admit, and once the furniture was in place the house felt a little less unfamiliar, even if that stain lingered somewhere in the back of his mind.

Sebastian had always been a meticulous man with everything having a place as he did not like upsetting the balance of his home with disorganization or disorder. He picked up the habit long before the Marines, but the Corps sharpened it until it felt second nature. If something was crooked or out of line, he noticed it right away, even when he tried not to. When people saw him, they usually took him for the typical gym rat. Most never guessed he preferred things quiet and simple, or that he kept order around him because it was the one thing that did not fall apart when life did. Discipline stuck with him more than anything else all thanks to his Marine service. With being two hundred pounds of pure muscle and standing at six foot seven it wouldn't be hard to see how they thought that, but the fact is he never visited the gym since he found the place repulsive so rather, he invested in his own equipment and ran on trails. People assumed the size came from endless hours in some warehouse-looking gym, but most days he preferred being outside where the air felt clean and no one was staring at him. He liked having his own space, his own pace, no music blasting in the background. Sebastian was never a man who could just sit still so he got himself a job at the local feed store helping farmers load their feed and other supplies into their trucks. It was not glamorous work, but it kept his hands busy and his mind quiet, and the farmers did not bother him much beyond a nod or a short story about weather or cattle.

Sebastian kept his life simple, spending his days either at the local library, working out, or working at his job at the local feed store. He liked the predictability of it, the way each day folded into the next without much noise or trouble. It was the first time in years he did not feel pulled in ten different directions at once. Sebastian began to be known to the locals as a gentle giant, never getting angry whenever someone got in his face or tried to provoke him. Some folks tested him now and then, more out of curiosity than meanness, and he would just stand there with that calm look that made people rethink whatever they were trying to prove.

Days had begun to pass with little to no changes in his day. The quiet felt strange at first, almost too still, but he got used to it because there wasn't much else to do. Sebastian kept a simple routine where he would wake up every morning at four in the morning. Old habits stuck, and even in a peaceful town his mind snapped awake before dawn like he was still waiting for some call that never came.

He would start his day off with a cup of coffee and a breakfast of eggs, bacon, and a bowl of oatmeal. The same meal every morning, the same way he cooked it, because it helped him feel settled. The smell of bacon in the pan always filled the kitchen before the sun even came up.

After breakfast he would go for a jog on the nearby trail and come home to pump out some reps on his workout bench. The trail was usually empty at that hour, just him and the sound of his footsteps and the cold air moving through the trees. It was the only time he really let his thoughts wander. Then one day, about two months after moving in, things started to slowly change. It was not dramatic at first, just small things he almost missed, but enough to make him pause in the middle of his routine and wonder if he had imagined it.

Even after he had settled into the routine of the place, there were these weird stretches of quiet that did not feel normal. These moments of quiet were not the peaceful kind by any means. It was the other kind. The kind where it felt like the walls were waiting on something.

Sebastian convinced himself that it was just an old farmhouse doing what old places do, shifting a bit whenever the wind changed. Even so, his gaze would drift toward the living room. Right to that spot under the couch where the stain was. He would not have admitted it to anyone much less another human being, but something about it bothered him. He did not have a good reason for it. Nothing in the room was different.

Nothing had been moved. Still, a small, unsettled feeling hung around, like whatever had been there had noticed him long before he ever thought to notice it.

CHAPTER 2

Over the next few mornings, Sebastian noticed that something in the house felt a little off, though he kept telling himself it was nothing. He had started seeing slight differences, like his speakers would no longer be symmetrical to his TV. His recliner would be at a forty-seven degree or forty-three degree offset no longer at its perfect forty-five degree offset. At first, he blamed himself, thinking maybe he had not paid attention the night before, but the more he looked at it, the more it bothered him. It felt like he was losing track of things he was usually sharp about, and that did not sit right with him.

He wasn't too concerned with it though, thinking maybe he had bumped into it at night or maybe he moved it without thinking about it. Whatever the case was, it began to upset the balance in his home causing him to be mildly annoyed with these things that began happening in his home. He kept trying to brush it off, but the little shifts stuck in his mind longer than he wanted. He knew how he left things, down to the inch, and it bothered him that he could not explain the changes. It felt like he was missing something obvious, and that small doubt stayed with him through the day.

He told himself he would drive to the nearby city to buy some surveillance cameras to find out who was moving his stuff around. He kept the idea in the back of his mind all day, telling himself he would get to it soon, but part of him hoped the whole thing would stop on its own.

However, it seemed his decision was a bit late to save him from the disaster to come. The next morning when he went to grab his favorite coffee mug, he found it shattered on the floor and upon seeing this it made him furious. He had that mug since he was a young Private First Class in the Marine Corps, back when he was going through basic training at Camp Pendleton.

Seeing it broken like that hit him harder than he expected. It was not the kind of thing he would usually get worked up over, but that mug had been with him through a lot, and now it was just bits of glass on the floor. For a second, he just stared at it, trying to make sense of how it ended up there in the first place.

He remembered the young woman who had sold it to him; the features of her face were something he'd never forget. Now it lay shattered on the floor. For a moment he just stood there, not moving, the memory of that day sitting heavier than he expected. It was not really about the mug, more about the time in his life it came from, and seeing it broken like that made him feel oddly off balance.

He grabbed the broom he kept nearby and cleaned the pieces of glass off the floor. He tried not to think too much while he swept, but the whole thing left him with a small, tight feeling in his chest that did not go away right away.

He then decided to continue his day with a level head, not letting this affect his attitude. He told himself it was just a rough start and tried to shake it off. But to his dismay he found that the bar to his bench press had been tampered with and was now missing one of the clamps. That stopped him for a second. He knew how careful he was with his equipment, and he would not have misplaced something as basic as a clamp.So now with his morning coffee and his morning routine messed up, he was beginning to lose his optimistic outlook. It was the kind of thing that normally would not bother him, but two problems back-to-back made the whole morning feel wrong in a way he could not quite explain.

So, he begrudgingly headed off to work. The whole drive felt longer than usual, and he caught himself replaying the morning in his head even though he kept trying to let it go. By the time he got to work, he was fifteen minutes late and was irritable. His boss, knowing that this was unusual for the usually peaceful Marine, called him into his office to talk to him. Sebastian could tell the moment he walked in that his boss had noticed something was off, and part of him felt embarrassed that a couple of small things at home had gotten under his skin this much.

As Sebastian talked about the things happening in his home, his boss listened and offered to help him in any way he could. Sebastian did not exactly go into dramatic detail, but he explained enough for his boss to pick up that something was not right at the house. It felt good just saying it out loud instead of letting it sit in his head all day. After talking with his boss, Sebastian felt better knowing that at least one man had his back if he needed anything. It was not much, but the reassurance steadied him a little.

After completing his shift, Sebastian decided to run over to the nearest town to buy a new clamp for the bar to his bench press and to check out surveillance cameras and see if he could get a decent deal on a good set.

After shopping around, he decided on getting two different types, one set being actual cameras while the other being easier to conceal from the naked eye. He was not thrilled about having to do all this, but at that point he wanted answers more than anything else, even if the whole situation still did not make sense to him.

After setting up the cameras in spots he knew would cover the largest areas he set off to bed. He checked each one twice, more out of habit than doubt, wanting to make sure he hadn't missed any angle. By the time he finally lay down, he was tired enough to hope the night would be quiet for once. He awoke in the middle of the night to a large thud and the sound of shattering glass. The sound snapped him upright before he even had time to think. He ran out of his room to try to catch whoever was doing it. His heartbeat was already up, not from fear exactly, but from that old instinct that kicked in whenever something felt wrong.

By the time he got to his kitchen there was no one around but in the middle of the kitchen lay a heap of glass from his coffee pot and several of his plates. The mess looked fresh, like it had only just happened, and he stood there for a second trying to make sense of how something that loud did not come with footsteps or movement. He rushed to his laptop where he had all the camera feed sent to so he could find out who had created the mess but was completely shocked when all he saw on the video was a black shadow throwing his stuff into the pile, shattering everything it threw. He replayed the clip twice, thinking maybe the screen had glitched or he was still half asleep, but the same dark shape moved the same way each time, silent and fast.

Angered that he had not caught the person that was messing with his life on video, he stormed into the kitchen to clean the mess that was left behind. He tried to focus on sweeping the glass, but his hands tensed up with every new piece he heard crack under the broom. Nothing about it felt right.

The next morning he was determined to stop the person causing all this, thinking it was some thief or a local kid that was bored and was looking to find their own entertainment. Telling himself that made the whole situation feel easier to handle, even if he was not completely sold on the idea.

He continued on his morning making coffee directly into his new mug since the pot had been shattered the night before. He did not like the change in routine, not one bit, but he tried to ignore the way it threw him off. He had decided during the night to act like nothing happened as he figured it would help him catch the culprit. So, he moved around the kitchen the same way he always did, pretending everything was normal even though the memory of the shattered glass still sat in the back of his mind.

He then decided to go about his regular routine of workouts before he then went off to work. He pushed through his sets the same way he always did, though he caught himself checking his equipment more than usual. When he got home that night, he was exhausted from pulling a double as his co-worker had called in sick. He expected the house to be in shambles from the intruder but was surprised to see the house was just as he left it.

The stillness hit him the moment he walked in, and for a second, he was not sure if that made him feel relieved or more on edge. Nothing being out of place almost felt stranger than the mess from the night before.

So naturally, he swept the rooms looking for something out of the ordinary. Yet he found nothing. So, he was in a better mood thinking that the intruder was done messing with him. Finally, he went off to take a shower so he could head to bed. Nothing else happened after that. The place did not make any noise, which felt strange but he did not want to get into it. He locked everything up and tried to stop thinking about how weird the day had been. He just wanted a quiet night and a normal morning for once.

CHAPTER 3

That particular night felt longer than the others. The house stayed quiet, but it was the kind of quiet that made him keep looking toward the doorway every now and then. He tried to brush it off and finally went to bed, hoping the morning would pull him back into his usual routine. But lying there in the dark, he could not shake the sense that something in the house was not settling the way it normally did.

As he lay in bed trying to wrap his head around the intrusions and why they haven't stolen anything from him he saw something out of the corner of his eye moving in his room. It was quick, just a blur near the edge of his vision, the kind of thing you doubt the second you notice it. He jumped out of his bed and grabbed his trusty Beretta out of the drawer in the nightstand and scanned his room but saw nothing. His pulse was already up, and he caught himself holding his breath without meaning to. The room looked the same as always, which somehow made it worse.

He stood there for a moment trying to slow his breathing down, the way he used to after night drills when his nerves got ahead of him. He kept the Beretta high as he swept the corners again, not rushing it. His eyes followed the same pattern he had used a hundred times before, but something about the room felt colder than it had a minute ago. He told himself he probably imagined the movement, maybe just a trick of the dark, but the gut feeling in his stomach did not back him up. The house felt too still, as if it was waiting on him.

So, he started sweeping his house from room to room trying to find what he saw in his room. He moved slowly, checking corners the same way he used to clear spaces overseas, though this time he had no idea what he was even looking for. As he started checking the living room his couch flew at him and he barely had time to drop to the floor before it flew past him and hit the wall just a foot behind him. The sound of it slamming into the wall was so loud it made his ears ring for a moment. He then jumped up ready to fire at his assailant. His grip tightened on the Beretta, and he kept his stance low, waiting for any sign of movement.

He moved down the hallway slower than he meant to, checking each doorway the way muscle memory taught him. His hands were steady, but his thoughts weren't. Every room he passed through felt wrong in small ways he couldn't name. A bit colder. A bit tighter. The air shifted once behind him and he turned fast, expecting footsteps, but nothing was there. For a second it reminded him of clearing abandoned compounds overseas, the moments right before something bad happened, when the silence felt too heavy. He tried to shake the thought off and kept going, but the feeling wouldn't leave him. Each breath sounded too loud in his own ears, and he couldn't help thinking none of this lined up with anything that made sense.

As he lined up his shot, he saw a black shadow coming at him so he fired three shots that just seemed to go through the black shadow. The rounds did not slow it down at all, and the noise in the room felt too loud for how little it seemed to matter. As he went to fire a fourth time he was lifted up off the floor and thrown into the wall. The hit knocked the breath out of him, and for a second, he could not move. As he tried to pick himself off the ground the black shadow seemed to have teleported next to him. He tried to swing at the shadow but hit nothing but air which shocked him to his very core. His brain could not make sense of swinging at something that looked solid but was not there when he touched it.

As soon as he managed to get his composure the black shadow disappeared and he decided that he had enough so he went to sleep in his truck till the morning when he could go to the library. He did not bother turning on any more lights or checking the rooms again; he just grabbed his keys and walked out because he could not stay inside that house another minute. He figured he put it off long enough and needed to know the history of the house. Whatever was happening in there was not something he could explain away anymore, and he knew he had to get some answers.

As soon as the sun came up, he headed to the library, stopping only long enough to get a cup of coffee at the local McDonald's. He felt drained from the night before, and the coffee did little to settle him, but it gave him something to hold onto while he tried to think straight. As soon as he got to the library he asked if he could see the history of the house that he was living in so he could understand what was happening because he knew whatever was happening wasn't normal. As he was flipping through the records on the house, he began noticing how no one ever lived there more than a couple of months and either moved out or left in a body bag. He read the pages twice just to be sure he was not mixing things up from lack of sleep, but the pattern was clear enough to make his stomach tighten.

When he finally found who the original owner was, and that they had died in the house he realized then what the stain was. It was the blood of the very first owner of the house, who died sixty years ago during a brutal home invasion. The intruders beat and tortured them until they finally shot them, leaving them to bleed to death slowly. Ever since, people had tried to get rid of the stain on the floor but had never been able to do it.

Seeing the details written out like that made the whole thing feel heavier. He kept staring at the short report, trying to picture how something like that could still hang around after so many years, and the more he read it, the more that old stain made sense in a way he did not want it to.

They had even ripped up the flooring and replaced it, adding carpet over it, but the stain still appeared. Seeing that written down made him sit back for a moment because he could not imagine how something could come back through brand-new flooring like it was nothing. So, Sebastian had made up his mind that he was going to call an exorcist to clear his home of this foul entity. It was not something he ever thought he would say out loud, but after what he had seen in that house, he did not feel like he had many options left.

So, he started looking around for the best exorcist and decided to go with a priest. His name was Father John, and he had stated he had cleared more homes of evil entities than any other exorcist. As Father John and Sebastian talked on the phone, Sebastian described the things that had been happening in his home and the history he had found on it. The priest had stated that he could cleanse the house of the evil entity, but it would be a major battle and he would need Sebastian there to help cleanse it. Hearing that made Sebastian pause for a moment. He was not sure what "a major battle" meant in this kind of situation, but after everything he would already seen, he did not argue. He just agreed, because he did not know what else to do anymore.

After the call ended, he sat in his truck for a while, trying to settle his thoughts. The idea of fighting something he could not touch or see the right way did not sit well with him, but he did not have a better plan. He just hoped the priest knew what he was talking about. By the time he headed home, he felt more tired than anything else, and all he could do was hope he would make it through the next day.

CHAPTER 4

The drive back to the house felt longer than usual, and the closer he got, the more he questioned whether calling a priest was going to fix any of this. He kept replaying what happened in the living room, the way the couch moved, the sound of it hitting the wall, the part where the shadow threw him like he weighed nothing. By the time he pulled into the driveway, all he could do was wait and hope Father John knew what he was walking into.

The night air felt thick to Sebastian as he waited for the Father to arrive. At exactly midnight he could see the Father's older, puke-green Nissan Maxima rumbling up the drive to his house.

As he watched the car crawl forward, he wondered why the man never bought something better and why he even chose that car in the first place, seeing how hideous it was to look at. The whole thing felt so out of place for what they were about to do that he almost laughed, but it came out more like a tight exhale. But Sebastian did not want to dwell on thoughts like that, as he needed to focus on the task at hand. He wiped his palms against his jeans and tried to keep himself steady, telling himself that midnight meant backup had finally arrived.

As the Father climbed the steps leading to Sebastian's front door, Sebastian could not help but notice the huge briefcase the Father was holding on to. The briefcase looked like it had seen better days; it had spots that had faded from what must have been black to a dull gray. The handle looked chipped and cracked, and there was a latch missing from the old briefcase. The whole thing looked like it had traveled through more trouble than the priest ever talked about. Sebastian caught himself staring at it for a second, wondering what he kept in there that needed a case that beat-up, but he pushed the thought aside. Tonight was not the night to start asking questions he was not ready for.

Sebastian thought that surely the old priest could have afforded a new briefcase with the money he earned. When the Father got up the steps, Sebastian stuck out his hand to shake his hand. The Father took Sebastian's hand and shook it with a firm handshake. For an older man, his grip was stronger than Sebastian expected, the kind that told you he had been doing this kind of work for a long time. Sebastian nodded once, still not sure what to say, and stepped back to let him inside.

Sebastian could not help but notice that the priest looked to be in his early sixties and how his hands felt like old, wrinkled leather. The man's hair was as white as snow, and he seemed to be balding at the top of his head. Yet the old priest seemed to have a warm smile and reminded Sebastian of his own grandfather before he passed away. There was something steady about the way he carried himself, the kind of quiet confidence older men sometimes had. It didn't erase Sebastian's nerves, but it made him feel a little less alone standing there in the doorway with him.

Sebastian asked what he was needed for, and Father John said he needed him to show him to the spot that he had mentioned on the phone. Sebastian led him toward the doorway slowly, trying to steady himself as they stepped inside. The house felt different the moment they crossed the threshold, he noticed it before he even had the chance to say anything. The air felt heavier, like someone had sucked the warmth out of the room. Father John paused for a second, his eyes drifting toward the hallway as if he picked up on it too. As soon as they walked into the house they both knew that the entity was not happy with them being there. It was almost like the entity knew what was about to happen. Sebastian felt the hairs on the back of his neck stand up, and he was not sure if it was fear or the temperature dropping again.

Sebastian took a slow breath and tried to steady himself the same way he used to before night patrol. It did not do much.

The house felt off now. Not just quiet, aware, almost, like it was paying attention to them. Father John hesitated before stepping closer to the stain, and Sebastian noticed how the man's eyes moved around the room in quick, careful sweeps. It was not fear. More like he recognized the kind of trouble this place could hold.

A small creak came from somewhere down the hallway. Both of them froze. The sound shouldn't have been there. It had the weight of somebody's step, just one, and just enough to make Sebastian's shoulders tense. His grip tightened around the flashlight without him thinking about it. Father John muttered something too soft to catch. The air shifted, colder, in a way that did not match the rest of the house, like the walls were breathing out frost.

For a moment, Sebastian thought about backing out and regrouping. Just a quick flash of doubt. But it faded just as fast. They were already here. Already past the point where turning around made sense.

When they reached the spot on the floor that Sebastian had told him about, the priest pulled out some holy water and sprinkled it on the spot and started reciting the Lord's Prayer. Sebastian watched him closely, feeling the air shift the moment the words left Father John's mouth. The floorboard under the stain seemed to creak even though neither of them had stepped on it, and a cold draft slid past Sebastian's shoulder like someone brushing by him.

As he started, he was violently thrown against the wall. The sound of the impact made Sebastian flinch hard. Sebastian, thinking the old priest was dead, jumped into action shielding the priest from harm, hoping he was not dead. He dropped to his knees beside him, one arm out, trying to block whatever had hit him even though he could not see anything in the room.

After a minute the priest stood up and started back with the Lord's Prayer. Sebastian could see his hands shaking a little, but Father John did not slow down. He caught his breath and went right back into the words like he had done this a hundred times before. The entity then started lashing out more violently, but Sebastian instinctively protected the priest, taking the blows that were meant to stop the priest. He felt the hits land on him, hard, sharp, almost like being shoved by something that was not fully there, and each one pushed him back a step. After the priest was done, he recited the Hail Mary prayer, which angered the spirit more, making him lash out in anger and pure hatred, trying to desperately get to the priest. But with Sebastian's big bulky body protecting the priest, it was difficult. He held his ground even when his legs shook from the force of it, refusing to let anything get past him.

When the priest finally started the last prayer, the entity was growing desperate, so in pure rage it threw Sebastian's recliner right at his head, forcing him to duck and giving the entity the opening it needed to get to the priest. Sebastian hit the floor hard, scrambling to get back up as the room shook from the force of the attack.

The entity picked up the priest to throw him, but it was too late. He finished the last prayer and threw the rest of the holy water at the stain on the floor, banishing the shadow. The moment the water hit the stain, the whole house seemed to pull in one long breath, and then everything went still.

Sebastian stayed on the floor longer than he meant to. He did not rush to stand. He just sat there trying to make sense of what even happened. His thoughts were all mixed up, kind of blurry. His ears had this faint ringing he couldn't explain. Maybe the chair hitting the floor did it. Maybe it was just him freaking out. Father John was next to him, bent over and sucking in air like he'd been running. He kept one hand on the wall, testing it almost, like he was not fully sure the place had settled down.

Sebastian looked at him, waiting for some kind of direction. Anything. A word would have helped. But Father John looked out of it too. His eyes were not focused. He stared past Sebastian for a couple of seconds, then blinked like he was trying to pull himself back into the moment.

The house turned quiet again. Not normal quiet. It felt heavier than before. The kind that makes you hold your breath without thinking about it. Sebastian pushed himself up. His ribs complained the whole way up. His shoulders felt stiff. Now that the rush was gone, every bruise he picked up decided to show itself.

He glanced at the stain. Part of him expected it to move or flare up or do something. Anything. It did not. It just sat there looking dull and unpleasant, like it had never been the center of whatever hit them a minute ago.

Father John finally stood straight. His face looked washed out, and he did not seem convinced about a thing, but he still said, "It's done." His voice did not land with much certainty. Sebastian nodded anyway, slow and unsure. A piece of him didn't buy it. Things that violent do not just stop clean. Not for him. Not ever.

For a few seconds, neither of them moved. Sebastian stayed crouched on the floor, waiting for something else to happen, but nothing did. The house did not shake, the air did not shift, and the cold that had been hanging around them was gone. Father John leaned against the wall to steady himself, looking exhausted but still alive. Sebastian did not say anything at first, he just tried to catch his breath and understand how close everything had come to going wrong. Whatever had been in the house was not there anymore, but the silence it left behind did not feel comforting. It felt like the kind that made you wonder what came next.

CHAPTER 5

The noise died, and the house went strange. Sebastian bent down, catching his breath, looking lost. Father John didn't speak. Sebastian didn't either. They just stood there with the kind of silence that follows something you can't rewind.

With the banishment of the entity, the house grew still and an eerie silence fell over the house. Sebastian was not used to this silence; there was always something going on in the house even before the entity started up.

Now the quiet sat heavy in the air, almost like the house was holding its breath. The old priest shook Sebastian's hand, thanked him for the protection, packed his belongings and left. Sebastian watched him as he walked down the stairs, got in his old puke-green Nissan, and headed down the drive, vanishing into the tree line.

For a moment Sebastian stood there, watching the taillights disappear, unsure if he felt relieved or just emptied out. Sebastian let out a deep sigh, walked back inside, and began the process of cleaning up. Every step felt slow, like his body had not quite caught up to what his mind was trying to process.

After a week of things being calm, Sebastian had finally got his house back in order with his recliner back at the perfect forty-five-degree angle offset to the TV and his two speakers symmetrical to the TV. He had started his routine again and even found a replica of his favorite mug.

Glad to have his life back to normal, he had a small celebration with a few of his friends. It felt strange at first having people over, but the noise and movement helped him forget about the way the house had looked during the exorcism. After things died down and everyone had left his house, he sat down in his recliner to watch some TV.

He began to doze off when he heard something, thinking maybe one of the house guests had stayed, so he got up to check. Only when he went to where he heard the noise, no one was there. The living room was exactly how he left it, too neat for anyone to still be inside. He began to look around, and that's when he noticed scratched into the side of the counter a message. The sight stopped him mid-step, the letters cut in deep enough to catch the light.

The message read "Thank you for freeing me." The words were carved deep, each letter uneven like whoever, or whatever, made them had no patience left. Panicked, he took a few steps back. Trying to calm himself, he took deep breaths and tried to reassure himself that it was a good message, meaning this would be the last thing he would hear from the entity. He kept repeating that in his head, but his hands still shook a little. Messages did not just appear out of thin air, especially not ones carved into wood.

Then he began to think about it and questioned how the entity did this if it was gone, which led him to think maybe the evil entity was imprisoning another here. The thought hit him slowly, the way bad realizations usually do. There had been two presences in the house... the violent one and something else he never fully understood. Maybe this entity was glad to be freed and would leave to find peace on the other side. He wanted to believe that. He really did. But standing there in the quiet kitchen, staring at fresh scratches that were not there an hour ago, he was not sure if peace had anything to do with it.

As another week had gone by without incident, he believed he was right that the entity that scribbled the message just wanted to thank him. The house felt normal again, the way it used to before everything started, and he let himself relax into that routine a little too easily. That is, until he began having nightmares. And since Sebastian had not had nightmares in nearly seven months, it was strange for them to start occurring again, especially since these nightmares weren't of the skirmish like he used to have.

These nightmares were strange and frequently woke him up, though he could never seem to recall what the nightmare was about or why it had woken him up. He always came out of them the same way, heart racing, throat tight, sweat on his forehead like he had been running. But he knew it had to have been a nightmare since he woke up screaming every time. The screams bothered him more than the dreams themselves. He had not screamed in his sleep since the early months after deployment, and the fact that it was happening again, without a single memory of the cause, made him uneasy in a way he did not want to admit.

After a few weeks of this recurring event, he decided to go see a doctor. The doctor said he was perfectly healthy and didn't show any reason for him having these nightmares. His mental state was perfectly healthy, and the only thing that stood out was him looking sleep deprived. So, they prescribed him something to help him sleep at night. Sebastian did not argue; he was too tired to explain the kind of fear that did not show up on charts. He had gone through evaluations before, years back, when the nightmares were tied to things he actually remembered, and those had been easier to talk about than whatever this was.

So that night Sebastian took the sleeping pills and dozed off to sleep for about four hours when he was violently awoken, but this time it was not from the nightmares. Sebastian was yanked out of bed and onto the floor by something, but did not know what, since the only thing that is ever been able to toss him like that was the entity which had been banished. He hit the floor hard, instinct kicking in before his brain caught up, the same way it had during old night raids when he woke up to someone shaking him out of a dead sleep. Only this time, there was no one there, just the echo of a force he should not have felt anymore.

He had seriously begun to think something was off, wondering if they did not truly banish the evil spirit but instead had been played a fool as it lay dormant. The thought crawled up slowly, the kind that sticks in the back of your head even when you try to shake it off.

Thinking that could not be the answer since even the stain had disappeared, and since the location of the stain was supposedly the entity's tie to the house, it could not possibly be around still. That was what Father John said. That was what he believed. Or could it be?

He stared at the spot where the stain used to be. Or where he thought it was. It was hard to tell now. The floor looked the same everywhere and his eyes were not helping. He kept looking anyway because he did not know what else to do.

His cheek started itching so he scratched it. Then his eyelid twitched. Felt like he had not slept at all. The room felt wrong. Not in a dramatic way. More like walking into a place you know and something is off but you cannot point at it.

He muttered to himself that he should just stop standing there. He did not move though. The weird feeling stuck to him. Like his body knew something and was not giving him the memo.

He sat on the bed. It sagged to one side and the shift annoyed him more than it should have. He tried fixing his position but it still felt lopsided. His feet hit the rug and the cold crawled up his toes. He wiggled them a bit. Habit maybe. Or nerves.

His eyes drifted around the room. Doorway. Dresser. The corner where the paint always looked a little darker. Nothing happened. Nothing made a sound. It was the same room but it did not feel like his.

He leaned forward, elbows on his knees. His breath slowed but his head felt busy. He kept going back and forth in his mind. Lie down or stay up. Neither sounded right. The bed felt off. The quiet felt worse.

Whatever woke him was not done with him. He felt that for sure. He was not sleeping again. So, he just sat there, staring at the floor like it might eventually tell him something.

CHAPTER 6

Early the next morning, Sebastian had decided to reread the article on the house to see if there was anything he had missed. Maybe he had accidentally skipped over a major detail or something. The thought would not leave him alone, and he kept going back to it in his head during the drive, replaying the pages he remembered and trying to picture the parts he skimmed too fast the first time.

So as soon as he arrived at the library, he sat down and skimmed the article, desperate to find out what he had missed. His foot tapped against the floor without him noticing, and every time he flipped a page his hands felt a little tighter than they should have. He was not sure if he was looking for information or just trying to reassure himself that there was a reason behind everything that had been happening.

He had spent two hours there when he made a huge discovery: the original owner wasn't one person but a family. The person who he assumed was a man that was tortured was actually a woman who was brutally tortured, raped, forced to watch as her two kids were shot in front of her eyes and then finally shot in the lower abdomen leaving her to bleed to death.

Sebastian read the lines twice, then a third time, thinking maybe he misunderstood something. His stomach tightened as he tried to picture the scene, and he wished he had not.

The culprit, as he tried to flee the house, ran into the husband who had just gotten off work, and when he tried to shoot the husband, he was knocked off balance and the gun went flying. Sebastian paused there, fingers resting on the edge of the page, trying to piece together how badly the whole thing must have unfolded. He felt a small pulse in his jaw as he gritted his teeth without meaning to, anger mixing with a sick sort of heaviness. This was not the kind of history you skim through.

The husband then beat the man to death and rushed inside to try to help his family, but when he got inside it was too late. His two kids lay on the floor with blood pooling beneath them, and his wife looked as if she were dead. Quickly, the husband grabbed the phone on the wall and called for help. He stood there crying, and then he heard a faint moan. Rushing back in, he saw that his wife was barely alive. She looked at her husband and asked if the culprit had gotten away, to which the husband said he didn't.

Sebastian slowed down as he read this part, his eyes sticking to the words longer than he intended. He could almost picture the scene, the panic, the shock, the way the husband must have stumbled back and forth not knowing who to touch first. He felt a tightness settle in his chest, the kind that comes from reading something you wish you had not opened yet can't look away from.

The wife then coughed, spitting blood everywhere, and simply said "Good. I'll make sure he never hurts anyone ever again." Then, with her last words said, she died. Sebastian stopped reading for a moment, trying to take in what she meant by that. The more he thought about it, the heavier it sat with him.

Sebastian remained completely mortified about what he read, he knew he got rid of the wrong entity. The entity he got rid of was only trying to keep him from releasing the true evil that lay in the house, and now it was free thanks to him. He felt the air drain out of his lungs, the kind of slow, sinking feeling you get when you realize you made a mistake you cannot undo. He closed the file and let himself fall back in the chair, staring ahead without really seeing anything.

He rubbed his hands over his face, trying to settle himself, but the room felt smaller than before. Everything he thought he understood about the house changed in an instant, and the new truth felt a lot worse.

The woman had not moved on. She had not been saved. She had been waiting. And now she was not trapped anymore.

Sebastian pushed back from the table, his chair scraping louder than he meant it to. He did not want to go home, but he did not have anywhere else to go. He just sat there a little longer, trying to figure out what he was supposed to do next.

CHAPTER 7

Sebastian walked out of the library with a twist in his gut. He did not even look around. Just headed for the car and sat there for a moment with the door still open. Felt like he needed air. Or water. Something.

He started driving but kept forgetting to pay attention to the road. The trip felt slow and weird, like the whole city stretched out. His head kept replaying the stuff he had read. Not in order. Just flashes. Bits that would not settle.

By the time he rolled into his driveway, he felt worn out in a way that did not match the length of the drive. He knew he was not sorting this on his own. That was not happening. Only one person he could even think of calling. And he did not love that idea either, because it meant saying out loud that both of them had messed this up from the beginning.

He sat there with the engine ticking, trying to figure out how to even start that conversation.

Flipping through his contacts, he found the number for the priest. He then called him, and in a panicked voice not known to Sebastian, he explained what he found. He kept talking fast, stumbling over parts of the story, trying to get it all out before he lost his nerve. The priest, realizing their mistake and how they read the entity wrong, said he would be back at Sebastian's place by midnight again.

Waiting at the end of the drive for the priest, Sebastian went over the details again in his head and how they had made a mistake. Every time he tried to calm his head, another line from earlier shoved its way back in. It all pressed on him the same way, right in the chest. He kept walking back and forth near the mailbox, not really going anywhere. Hands in his pockets, then out again. He could not stay still. The whole time he had this slow, sinking feeling that they had missed their window and were already behind.

As he was waiting, he saw the old puke-green Nissan clambering up the small hill that lead to Sebastian's driveway. The sight of it made his shoulders loosen a little, even if only for a second. Excited to know that the true evil would soon be banished, he climbed back in his truck and drove down the rest of the driveway with the old Nissan following him.

By the time they got to the house, he knew something was wrong. The front door was left wide open like it was beckoning them to come inside. Sebastian felt a small jolt in his gut when he saw it – no wind, no reason for it to be open, and he was sure he had closed it earlier. He locked eyes with Father John, and without saying a word, they nodded, braced for whatever was about to happen, and went inside.

When they entered the house, it looked like someone had detonated a bomb inside. Chairs were flipped, dishes lay shattered on the floor, the TV was thrown violently against the wall, and there in the middle of all this stood a man with his head hung low. Sebastian froze for a second, trying to make sense of the shape of him, the way he stood completely still even with the wreckage around him. The man slowly raised his head, and that's when they saw the distorted face with what seemed to be a huge smile. It was the kind of smile that looked wrong on a human face, too wide, too tight, like it had been pulled into place instead of formed naturally.

The door then slammed shut, and they knew they were trapped in there with it. The sound hit hard enough to make Sebastian flinch, and the air in the room seemed to tighten right after. The priest grabbed his holy water and went to throw it at the entity, but he was stopped mid-swing and thrown against the wall. The impact knocked a grunt out of him, and Sebastian took a half-step forward before catching himself.

The entity chuckled, and in a low, hoarse voice said, "You know, I should truly thank you for freeing me from my wife."

Shocked, Sebastian asked, "I thought you'd be the thief. Why would she keep her husband prisoner?" His voice came out tighter than he intended, part confusion, part anger, trying to understand what he was even talking to.

The entity let out a terrifying laughter and then stated, "The police in this town have always been poor detectives. I caught my wife cheating on me when I came home early that day. I caught him and beat him to a bloody pulp, then I busted down our front door and dragged my wife out of the room. I tied her to a chair and beat her until she was barely recognizable."

Sebastian felt his stomach twist as he listened, the way you do when someone says something so cruel that your mind struggles to line it up with a human face. He glanced at Father John, who was still trying to get his breath back, then looked at the distorted figure again, trying to understand how anyone could talk about something like that without a shred of hesitation.

"After that, knowing she could still see, I dragged our kids in the living room and made her watch as I shot both of them in the head. Then I shot her in her abdomen so I could state she was still barely alive when I got home. But that harlot cursed me with her dying breath and trapped me in this damn house forever."

With this news, Sebastian became furious at the entity for what he had done. His hands tightened at his sides, and he felt a sharp heat rise in his chest as the truth settled in. Sebastian rushed over to the priest to help him up, but then the entity sliced the priest's throat open, spewing blood all over Sebastian. Sebastian froze for a split second, shocked by how fast it happened, the warmth hitting his face before his mind caught up with the sight in front of him.

CHAPTER 8

Sebastian did not remember getting back to his feet. Everything after the priest's fall was a blur, the sound, the movement, the way the room tilted. His mind kept slipping between shock and confusion, and for a second, he could not even feel his own hands. The house felt smaller, tighter, like the air itself was pressing down on him.

Horrified about what had just happened and not knowing what to do, Sebastian crumpled over the priest's body. His knees hit the floor harder than he expected, and for a moment he could not make himself look at the wound. He just tried to breathe, tried to get a thought in order, but nothing lined up.

Laughing at the once mighty Marine, the entity looked at Sebastian and said, "Oh how the mighty have fallen. You used to be so high and mighty. A hero to this country, but now look at you, a worthless scum trembling in fear of me."

Sebastian forced down a breath, his jaw was completely clenched when the words finally registered in his mind. He did not answer, not because he agreed, but because he could not trust his voice to come out steady. His hands hovered uselessly over the priest's shirt, not sure where to touch or what to fix, knowing it did not matter anymore.

That's when the entity realized too late what Sebastian had been playing at. Sebastian had been clutching the small bottle the whole time, his hand shaking but steady enough to aim. He threw holy water right into the face of the still-smiling entity.

Hearing the water sizzle off the man's face, Sebastian leapt to his feet and tried to battle the entity by repeating the Lord's prayer, but the entity had enough. The words came out rushed and uneven, like he was trying to catch up to himself. He did not even know if he was saying them right anymore.

He lifted Sebastian off his feet by his throat, and the entity growled out the words, "Since you freed me, I will let you live. But if you come back, I won't be so nice."

Sebastian clawed at the hand around his neck, trying to get some kind of grip, but his fingers kept slipping. He could not get air in, just short, broken breaths that did not help at all. His vision started to shake from the pressure.

With that the entity threw Sebastian out the window and onto his truck. The glass burst around him as he hit the hood, the impact knocking the wind out of him so fast he did not even hear himself land. He stayed there for a second, trying to figure out where the sky was and where the truck ended.

Wincing from the pain, Sebastian did not know which was worse, the landing or the broken glass that had cut his skin. Every breath felt sharp, and when he tried to move his arm, the sting shot up higher than he expected. He sat there for a bit, just trying to steady himself.

After a while, Sebastian was able to pick himself up and called the police, not knowing what else to do. When they arrived, they found Sebastian hunched over his arm, trying to pull out a long piece of glass that was lodged deep beneath the skin. The shard pressed up just enough to lift the torn flesh around it, and every time he gripped it with his fingers a thin line of blood rolled down his wrist. He kept working at it anyway, breathing through his teeth, trying to get enough leverage to pull it free.

The edges of the glass scraped against the wound each time he tugged, making the skin pull and stretch in a way that turned his stomach. He was shaking more from frustration than fear, determined to get it out himself, until one of the officers stepped forward and told him to stop before he tore the skin open any further.

They put Sebastian into an ambulance and asked if anyone else was inside and what happened. He stared at them for a second, trying to come up with something that made sense, but nothing he said would've sounded right, not even to himself.

Sebastian, not knowing how to explain what had happened, decided to avoid the real answer and just told police there was another body inside.

He told them it was the body of Father John, to which the police officers responded by asking could possibly be in the house that could've killed Father John. Sebastian looked away at that, jaw stiff, because he did not have anything to give them. He just felt the question hang there, heavier than the pain in his arm.

Shocked by this question, Sebastian finally decided to tell them everything. The words came out in short pieces at first, like he had to force each part through his throat. He kept glancing at the floor of the ambulance, unable to look at the officers for more than a second at a time. When Sebastian finished telling them everything, they seemed shocked, but they still needed to recover the body of the old priest, so they decided to gather their courage up and went into the house.

Sebastian watched them from the back of the ambulance, his fingers digging lightly into the stretcher beside him. Part of him wanted to warn them again, to say something else, but nothing useful came to mind. They were going in no matter what he said.

When they got inside, it was eerily silent, so they pressed on into the living room where they found the priest strung up to the wall in what looked to be a mockery of a crucifixion. His arms were pulled wide at angles no living body could hold, shoulders slumped forward like they had been forced into place. Dried streaks of blood ran down both sides of his torso in uneven lines, turning his shirt into something stiff and dark. His head hung low, chin resting against his chest, and the skin around his neck looked stretched from the way he had been positioned, like something had pinched and lifted him rather than placing him there. The whole scene looked wrong in a way that made the officers freeze where they stood. Both officers stopped at the doorway, neither one stepping forward at first, as if their minds needed a second to catch up with what they were seeing. Carved in his body was a message that read "You will never leave this place."

One officer let out a shaky breath, the kind that slips out when you are trying not to react too loudly. The other reached for his radio with a stiff hand, eyes locked on the message like he did not trust himself to look away. They did not say anything to each other. They just stood there a moment, taking in the quiet and everything it meant.

CHAPTER 9

Sebastian tried to sit up in the ambulance when he heard shouting, but the pain in his arm kept him down. He could still see the house from where he lay, the lights from the officers' flashlights bouncing around inside the broken doorway. Then everything went quiet at once, and that sudden quiet settled in his chest like a warning.

As soon as they saw this message, an eerie laughter rang throughout the house. It came from nowhere at first, bouncing off the walls in a way that made it impossible to tell where the source was. Both officers snapped their heads up, staring into the dark like they expected someone to step forward. The doors then slammed shut, and the police officers realized they were trapped, so they all began to kneel and pray.

About that time, the priest started moving and flew off the wall, ripping his hands free from the nails that held him to the wall. The sound of the nails tearing loose made one officer gasp, his hand flying instinctively to his mouth. The priest's body hit the floor in a way that didn't sound right, limbs landing stiff and heavy, like whatever was moving him wasn't concerned about the form it was using.

The dead priest came over in a horrifying shamble dragging his right foot behind him. Each step sounded wrong, the heel catching slightly before scraping forward again. When he got to the police officers who were kneeling and praying, he raised his hand and went to swing at them.

The priest was stopped mid swing by a huge, burly arm. Looking up, they saw Sebastian standing tall with his teeth gritted. His face was tight with anger and strain, not hesitation. He apologized to the old priest as he knocked him off his feet and slammed him into the ground. The impact rattled the floor hard enough to make the walls shudder.

Sebastian slammed his shoulder into the nearest door, breaking it into two. Wood split and cracked outward as he forced it open. The police officers were hot on Sebastian's heels, trying to stay close enough so they wouldn't be separated from the big, burly Marine. Neither of them dared to look back.

As they rushed through the house, objects flew at them from all directions. Something hard clipped the wall beside Sebastian's head, and another object spun past his shoulder close enough that he felt the air move. One of the officers cried out when a sharp piece sliced into his arm, blood spotting his sleeve as he stumbled but kept moving.

They eventually reached the front door, and Sebastian rammed it with the remainder of his strength. Pain flared through his shoulder, but he did not slow down. The door shattered on impact, wood breaking apart as everyone spilled outside, escaping the house and the entity that lay inside. None of them stopped running until they were clear of the porch, breathing hard, afraid to look back at the open doorway behind them.

Gasping for air, Sebastian collapsed to the ground, his lungs burning like they had been set on fire.

His shoulder felt shredded and, the pain told him right away that he had reopened the old wound there. He clenched his teeth and rolled slightly onto his side, trying to get his breathing under control, every inhale feeling shallow and useless. He cursed the sniper that shot him, wishing he never got hit in the first place, but he knew it was just a fact of life and something he couldn't avoid. That kind of thinking never lasted long anyway.

By the time he was able to get to his knees, the police officer who had his arm sliced open was already being treated, and the paramedics were trying to get Sebastian on his feet. Hands grabbed at his arms and shoulders, voices overlapping as they told him to stay still. He nodded without really listening, still focused on the pain and the house looming behind them.

The sun started to peak over the horizon by the time Sebastian had gotten all of his wounds checked out, and the more serious ones were treated and given the okay. The light felt wrong after everything that had happened, see-through and too calm for what the night left behind. They still had no clear way of retrieving Father John's body or how to cleanse the home of the foul entity.

Sebastian felt like he was at a complete loss. If he could not get rid of this entity, he'd lose everything and end up homeless. The thought hit harder than the pain in his shoulder. He looked back toward the house once more, knowing he couldn't go back inside and not knowing where that left him.

He had nowhere left to turn. He felt like this was it, and the only man who knew how to cleanse the house was dead and might even be stuck there forever. The weight of that thought settled in slowly, heavier than the night had been.

Sebastian, for the first time in his life, felt hopeless. It was not panic or fear the way he was used to. It was the kind of empty feeling that comes when you run out of options and don't see another door to kick in. As he watched the tow truck start to pull away with the priest's puke-green Nissan, Sebastian had a thought – maybe even a plan.

It wasn't a good one. It wasn't clean. But it was something. And right now, something was better than standing there waiting for the house to take whatever it wanted next.

CHAPTER 10

Sebastian stood there watching the tow truck roll a few more feet before he finally moved. The thought wouldn't let go, and the longer he let it sit, the worse it felt. He didn't know if it was instinct or desperation, but he knew one thing for sure, letting that car disappear felt like another mistake he couldn't afford to make.

Sebastian, knowing he needed to stop the tow truck, asked one of the cops if they could stop it for him. The cop, curious as to why, asked, "Why do you want us to stop the tow truck from taking the priest's car?"

Sebastian explained that he noticed when the priest entered the house all he had on him was the holy water and not the old briefcase that the priest was known to carry. He kept his voice steady as he said it, but his mind was already racing, replaying the image of Father John walking up the steps with that case in his hand. If the briefcase wasn't inside the house, then it had to be somewhere else. And if it was still out there, then maybe not everything Father John knew was lost with him.

So the cop stopped the tow truck and let Sebastian try to find the briefcase. The driver watched him from the side, arms crossed, while Sebastian moved around the car slower than he wanted to, afraid of missing it if he rushed. After a bit of searching, he found it, and when he grabbed it he noticed an envelope tucked behind the old briefcase.

When he looked at the envelope, he noticed in a neat, and almost flawless handwriting was the address to Sebastian's home. That made his stomach drop. He stared at it longer than he meant to, tracing the numbers with his eyes, knowing Father John must have written it for a reason.

Curious about what the envelope held, Sebastian grabbed it along with the briefcase. The weight of the case felt heavier than he expected, like it carried more than just what was inside. Looking at it closer, he realized the crack in the handle = = was a lot bigger than he first thought. He also noticed that the remaining latch looked like it used to be a gold, now dulled with age. Right above the latch, on a faded gold plate, was the priest's name, barely visible to the naked eye.

He opened it up, hoping to find some clear answer on how to rid the house of the entity, but all he found was a notepad, three pencils, a bottle of holy water, and a bible. At first, it felt like nothing. Then it settled in that Father John hadn't carried solutions. He'd carried preparation.

Not sure what to do with it, Sebastian turned his attention to the letter. He wasn't sure if he should open it, and after a moment he handed it over to the police, reluctantly. Letting it leave his hands felt wrong, but he couldn't explain why without sounding unhinged. The police took it and decided that it should be filed as evidence related to the whole event.

They took the briefcase as well, since Sebastian had no use for its contents. Watching it disappear into the back of the cruiser, left a hollow feeling in his chest. Stuck back at square one, he felt like there had to be something he was missing, something just out of reach, but he could not put his finger on it.

So he went over all the details again in his head and tried to remember the three prayers the priest had used to banish the first entity, but could only recall two of them. The third stayed just out of reach, no matter how hard he pressed for it.

Deciding he needed answers, he went online and searched for the prayers used to exorcise houses and rid them of evil entities.

After searching for a solid ten minutes, he finally found what he was looking for. The three prayers used to cleanse a home were the Lord's Prayer, Hail Mary and the Athanasian Creed. Seeing the words laid out like that made his stomach tighten. This was not guesswork anymore. Determined to rid his home of the evil entity and save the priest who had helped him, he grabbed some holy water and decided he would march back inside the home.

Around noon, Sebastian started sprinkling holy water into the front room and started walking inside. Knowing he was heading into a major fight, he braced himself, shoulders tight, ready for the worst. Nothing happened. The house didn't react at all, and that almost bothered him more. He kept moving, sprinkling holy water as he went, deeper into the house.

When he reached the room where he had left the priest lying on the ground, it felt like he was trudging through thick mud. Each step took more effort than it should have, his boots dragging slightly as if the floor itself didn't want him there. When he went to sprinkle holy water in the room, he heard the same eerie laughter he had heard before. He knew who it was.

In a loud, steady voice, Sebastian declared "I'm not afraid of you. No matter what you do to me, I will stand strong." The laughter continued for another minute or two, slow and patient, before he heard a sound coming from the corner of the room.

It was the priest, or what used to be him, shambling toward Sebastian. The body moved wrong, stiff in some places and loose in others, like it wasn't being guided by muscle anymore.

The priest stopped a few feet away and said, "Do you know why I killed the priest, instead of throwing him out the window like I did you?" The voice was eerie and distorted, and Sebastian knew it wasn't Father John speaking.

Sebastian replied "Because he was trying to get rid of you for what you did to your family."

The priest let out a harsh cackle. "No," he said. I killed him because he stunk of that harlot's lover. He was the son of that wretched man I claimed was the thief."

Sebastian froze. The words didn't make sense at first, then all at once they did. He had never once considered that the priest could be tied to the house or its history. The thought left him off balance, and the entity didn't waste the moment.

It surged forward and grabbed Sebastian by the throat, lifting him off his feet. The hands felt dry and leathery, too strong for a body that old. Sebastian's thoughts scattered as the grip tightened, his chest burning as the air was slowly forced out of him.

With what little energy he could muster, Sebastian splashed holy water into the face of the old priest. The reaction was immediate. The skin darkened and blistered where the water hit, smoke curling up as the entity let out a furious scream.

Enraged, it threw Sebastian into the wall hard enough to knock the air from his lungs. Before he could recover, it grabbed him again and slammed him into the ground. Pain flashed white behind his eyes, and for a split second he was sure this was it. This was how he was going to die.

Then the entity hurled him through the window. Glass shattered around him as he flew outside, his body skipping across the ground like a stone across water before finally coming to a stop. He lay there stunned, breath ragged, staring up at the sky, knowing the house had beaten him again, but not finished with him.

CHAPTER 11

Sebastian blinked hard, the bright sky above him blurring in and out of focus. The shock had settled in, but the pain still hadn't caught up to him yet. He felt like he was still in motion, still being thrown around even though everything had stopped. But he couldn't stay here. Not now.

Sebastian hit his truck, stopping himself from bouncing further. The lurch went straight to his chest, and he groaned, not sure if it was the truck's impact or his own body fighting to stay together. As Sebastian lay there, looking up at the sky, he started wondering how much more abuse his truck could take. He already knew he had reached his limit.

The front bumper was bent, and something in the engine had to be messed up by now. He was pretty sure he had at least three broken ribs and no telling how many more broken bones in the rest of his body. Every breath felt sharp, like his lungs were being squeezed tighter with each inhale. He could feel the pain starting to settle in, but there was no time to think about it. The next thing had already started.

Sebastian couldn't help but think about his days in the Marines and all that he had accomplished. He tried not to dwell on it, but the memories slipped in anyway, training, missions, the camaraderie of the men who fought beside him. He then thought of the days he had spent fighting for his life, and how many times he thought, *this was it – this is how I'll die.* But somehow, he always made it through.

Each close call still sat with him, but the thought didn't paralyze him like it used to. He'd always come out on the other side, battered, sure, but alive. But now? Now he felt something different. He wasn't sure he'd make it this time.

He even went as far as to think that maybe he thrived in those kinds of situations. Maybe that's why he was eager to rush headfirst into the house without having a true plan. The thrill of it, maybe, or the belief that he could handle whatever came his way. But now, as he lay on the ground, broken, bruised, and battered, he tried thinking up a plan. But nothing was coming to mind. His thoughts kept slipping away like sand through his fingers.

The only thought that came to mind now was how he was going to get out of this situation since he told no one of what he was about to do. He had never felt so alone in a fight, and the sheer burden of that made everything feel worse.

Just then, a shadow came over him, blotting out the sun. Sebastian's first thought was that this was it, that the entity had come out of the house to finish him off. He accepted his fate, everything that had happened till then came crashing in at once like tidal wave, and for a moment he let go of the fight.

As he lay there, waiting for the final blow, he looked up once again to see a girl who seemed extremely happy, with a smile on her face. She was standing there in the light, not quite a shadow, but not fully in the world either. He didn't know who she was or why she was here, but for the first time in what felt like forever, he was grateful. Maybe she was here to help, to pull him out of this nightmare before it swallowed him whole.

The girl leaned over him and checked on him, making sure he was alive. After that, she called someone over to help her. Sebastian barely registered the movement, his vision was still blurry and his body too weak to respond properly. He managed to ask, "Who are you, and why are you here?"

She looked at him with a strange mix of relief and concern, then said, "My name is Charlotte, and I was sent here to look for you by the police. You've been missing for three days, and we assumed we would find your corpse."

Sebastian blinked, trying to make sense of the worlds. Three days? How could it have possibly been three days when he had just gone into the house and only an hour or so ago? The time did not add up. His mind scrambled to find an explanation, but before he could ask another question, everything around him went dark.

Spirit looked at the now still Marine, wondering how her and her partner would ever manage to get him off the ground. He was heavier than he looked, and his body was limp, almost unnaturally so. But more importantly, she couldn't help but be mesmerized by him. He had run headfirst into a house that was controlled by an extremely evil entity just to save his house and a priest that he barely knew.

She admired that kind of courage, but it felt like something she'd never fully understand. But she had to focus on the task at hand. With her partner's help, they managed to get him to their car and lay him down on the back seat.

As they headed for the nearest hospital, she could hear him stirring, and she feared he would panic when came to and hurt himself. Her heart raced as she watched his chest rise and fall with each shallow breath. She asked her partner to speed up and get to the hospital faster. She didn't know how much longer he could stay unconscious without making things worse.

By the time they got to the hospital and got him on a gurney, he had come to – and indeed, panicked. Not knowing where he was, he tried to fight back, but was quickly sedated to keep him from doing any more harm to himself or the staff. The feeling of helplessness set in fast, and even with the sedatives, he struggled against it for a few seconds longer than he should have.

When the hospital finally got done with all the tests and got the full extent of his injuries, they were shocked he was still able to put up any fight. The bruises were just the start. Every time they moved him, another injury was revealed.

Sebastian had five fractured ribs, every bone in his right arm was either shattered, fractured or cracked; he had a fracture in his left femur; his left hand was completely shattered, with no bones left intact. His left shoulder was dislocated; his right one had a fracture and torn ligament in it; his left hip had a massive labral tear, and he had various cuts and bruises, some being more severe, needing immediate attention. The doctors were silent for a moment, running over the list of injuries again in disbelief. Sebastian, barely conscious, couldn't feel most of it, but the weight of the report made his head spin.

Yet he still had a fight in him, trying desperately to get up and get back to the fight he had been dealing with for the past month or two. Sebastian's body shook with the effort, the pain lighting up every nerve, but his mind kept pushing forward, fighting against the stillness of the bed.

Charlotte looked at Sebastian lying in the hospital bed and thought to herself how even this man, who used to be two hundred pounds of pure muscle, was now lying on the bed, broken, unable to move without pain. She couldn't help but notice how much smaller he looked now, how the fight in him felt so different from the one she had seen before.

Charlotte knew that the only way to get him to finally be at peace was to finish what he started, but she needed him. They couldn't do this alone. She and her partner had tried everything they could, but without Sebastian, it felt like they were running blind. She and her partner alone couldn't fight off the entity, and she knew it. So she decided the only option was to wait for Sebastian to fully heal up.

Charlotte sat by the window, watching the rain start to fall outside, her mind racing through every option they had left. The house, the entity, everything was still waiting. She glanced back at Sebastian, still unconscious, his breath steady but slow. It felt like time was working against them, and she knew they didn't have the luxury of waiting much longer. She took a deep breath and steadied herself. No matter how long it took, they'd finish this, but only when Sebastian was ready. And for now, that meant waiting.

CHAPTER 12

It took Sebastian six months to fully heal from the surgeries he went through, and another four months to fully rehabilitate, to be able to use his hand, arms, and his left leg again. The first few months felt like endless days of pain, his body still fighting to remember what it used to be able to do. But eventually, he found some semblance of normal again.

Soon after, he was approached by Charlotte. She asked him, "Will you help me finish what you've started?"

Sebastian looked at her, remembering her face and how they'd met. He smiled at her, but the smile didn't reach his eyes. "No," he said softly, his voice tired, "I've had enough. I'm done fighting the entity."

Charlotte looked at him, searching his face, then asked, "What about the priest? Would you really leave him to that fate? To become the entity's puppet?"

Sebastian met her eyes, and she saw the answer in them before he said a word. There was no fight left in him, no resolve. She could feel the weight of his exhaustion, the way his shoulders had dropped from what they once were. He truly was broken – maybe beyond repair. The entity had won. It had shattered his will, and now, she stood in front of the shell of the Marine he used to be.

Sebastian left the hospital and went to look at an apartment he had inquired about the day before. The walk from the hospital to the apartment was quiet, and he felt strangely disconnected from everything around him, like the world was moving at a pace he was not part of anymore.

Two weeks later, after hearing nothing from Sebastian, Charlotte began to worry if Sebastian was okay. So, she went to his new apartment to check on him. When she knocked, the big, burly Marine answered the door. He smiled at her and invited her inside. His face looked unchanged, but there was something different in the way he held himself, smaller, almost defeated.

When she came in, she was shocked at what she saw. Inside Sebastian's apartment were newspaper clippings about the murder of the family, the history of the house, and there were even clippings and records of the priest. The walls were covered, like some kind of map, each piece carefully pinned in place but adding up to something chaotic, as if Sebastian was trying to make sense of a puzzle that didn't fit.

Not knowing what to think or say, she just stared in both awe and confusion. Her mind raced, trying to understand why someone so broken would go back to this, to the thing that had nearly torn him apart. When Sebastian finally snapped Charlotte out of her daze, she looked at him and asked, "What's with all this stuff, I thought you had given up and didn't want anything else to do with the entity or the house."

Sebastian just shrugged and said he couldn't just quit halfway through a mission, and that it didn't feel right condemning someone to be a puppet to an evil being. His voice was flat, almost like he was trying to convince himself as much as Charlotte.

As Charlotte and Sebastian talked, he revealed what he learned about the priest and what actually happened to the family. The more he spoke, there was no getting around what had gone wrong.

When Sebastian got up to get them a refill on their drinks, Charlotte sat mesmerized by how a man could take so much abuse from something and still be able to face it in defiance. The thought of that kind of strength made her feel small, like she had no right to ask what kept him going, yet she could not stop wondering.

As she sat there, wondering about him and everything he was doing, she noticed a photograph out of the corner of her eye. Curious as to what it was, she walked over to it and looked at it. The photo was old, edges were frayed, but the faces in it seemed as clear as day. She noticed 8 men standing beside each other. She then recognized one of them as Sebastian.

As she was examining the photo, she didn't hear Sebastian walk up behind her. So when he put his hand on her shoulder, she jumped, nearly dropping the photograph onto the floor. Sebastian chuckled a little and apologized for scaring her. In return, she apologized for being nosy.

Sebastian just shrugged and said he did not mind, that the photograph was just him and his buddies from the Marines. He picked it up carefully, his fingers running over the edges as if he was used to it, but there was a softness to his touch that made Charlotte notice how much he valued it.

He then made a joke about if they were here and saw him get his butt kicked by an entity, they'd probably laugh at him and make jokes. The corner of his mouth pulled into a smile, but it didn't reach his eyes.

She asked, "Where are they now? Did they leave the service when you did?"

After she said that, sadness washed over Sebastian, and he said "Kinda. They were all killed in the last skirmish we were in."

His voice dropped at the end, quiet but heavy. His eyes shifted downward for a second, his hand running through his hair like he was trying to keep himself together. "I was the sole survivor of it, and honestly, I doubt I was supposed to make it out either."

Shocked at what she just heard, Charlotte didn't know what to say. Her mouth opened slightly, then closed again. The words felt stuck in her throat, as if they could never be enough to fix the silence between them. She just stood there in silence, trying to find what to say.

Sebastian just smiled, a small, tired thing. "It's in the past. We need to focus on the task at hand." His voice sounded like it had been worn down by time, his posture pulling in slightly as if the weight of his own words pressed against him.

With that, Sebastian turned and headed for the table. Charlotte stood there for a moment, the photo still in her hands, feeling the weight of what she had just heard. It was like she had opened a door into a part of his life she had no right to walk into, but couldn't look away from.

Charlotte set the photo back down on the counter, but her mind stayed on the quiet pieces of Sebastian's past. She knew better than to ask any more questions, but she also knew that whatever they were facing in that house, it wasn't just going to be something they could fight with holy water and prayers.

Sebastian had already fought too many battles to let this one be any different. But the difference now was that he wasn't the only one going in. Charlotte knew, just like him, that they couldn't do it alone. They never had. But she could see now that whatever was left of Sebastian after everything he had been through, that was the part that still had to fight.

The air in the room felt heavier somehow, like the real battle was just beginning, and there was no turning back.

CHAPTER 13

After they were done talking about the photograph of his squad, Sebastian set the frame back down on the counter. He leaned against the wall, his eyes scanning the chaotic map of newspaper clippings he had pinned up earlier. He turned to Charlotte and asked her for a favor, specifically regarding a piece of information he felt would help solve the missing piece of the puzzle.

The piece of information that he needed was the letter that he had found tucked behind the priest's briefcase. Sebastian paced the small living room of his new apartment, favoring his left leg slightly—a habit picked up during his rehabilitation. He knew there had to be a reason the priest had left it in his car but he had no idea why. He stopped pacing and looked at Charlotte. All he knew is that he needed Charlotte to get it so he could find out what was inside. Charlotte stood by the door, watching him. She knew that Sebastian was going to find a way to get it anyway, perhaps by storming down to the station himself, so she decided to help him get it to keep him out of trouble.

As she went into work the next morning, Charlotte didn't go to her desk. She walked straight down the hallway to the administration wing. Charlotte walked into the chief's office and asked if she could give the letter to Sebastian stating that they had no use for it and it did technically belong to Sebastian as it had his address on it.

The police chief listened, leaning forward with his elbows on his desk. When Charlotte was done explaining her reasoning to him he just sat there thinking. He swiveled his chair slightly, staring at the file cabinets against the wall. He sat there thinking about the dilemma he had in front of him, one that for the first time in his twenty six years in service to the city he had no answer to.

As the chief sat there thinking about the answer, he rubbed his temples slowly. Charlotte couldn't help but notice that the chief had really started looking his age. Under the harsh office lights, the lines on his face looked deeper. His mustache had started graying around the edges and he even had gray flecks all through his hair.

Lost in thought, she was startled when the chief stopped rubbing his temples and began to speak saying "I think that you're right the letter does technically belong to Sebastian and as it does us no good in trying to find a solution on how to get the priest's body out of the house I suppose you can give it to him."

Glad that she had gotten the letter with no issues she thanked the chief and walked to the evidence room to retrieve the letter for Sebastian. She signed the logbook, took the plastic evidence bag containing the envelope, and slid it into her jacket pocket before heading for the exit.

After her shift Charlotte went over to Sebastian's apartment to check on him and to give him the letter. When she got there she found Sebastian studying the clippings he had about the priest's past. He was standing close to the wall, tracing a line between two articles with his finger. He looked tired, but his focus was sharp.

She looked at Sebastian and held the letter out to him and said "I've got the letter for you to open whenever you're ready."

Sebastian turned towards her with a smile and thanked her for the letter. He took it from her hand and opened it carefully so he didn't damage the envelope or the letter inside. He pulled out the single sheet of paper and unfolded it. Sebastian, deciding that Charlotte would want to know what the letter said, cleared his throat and began to read it aloud so she could hear. The letter reads;

Dear Sebastian,

I hope this letter finds you well as I know if you're reading this then my time is up in this world. The first time I came to your

When Sebastian finished reading the letter he lowered the paper. He looked at the names on the page one last time, and then he folded the letter carefully, as if putting it back together might somehow steady what it revealed.

He asked if Charlotte wanted to join him to find the two Fathers that Father John had mentioned in his letters.

She didn't even think about it for a split second, and agreed ecstatically.

She grabbed her keys from the table and nodded, ready to leave right then and there.

CHAPTER 14

The next day, Charlotte called the chief and ask for a few days off. He agreed without hesitation, she had the sense that he'd been expecting the request.

So, with the clearance from the chief, Sebastian and Charlotte immediately began searching for Father Carlos and Father Sean. What started as a methodical effort quickly became exhausting. They combed through parish records, dioceses, and Catholic churches across the state and beyond, following lead after dead end until the hours blurred together. For Sebastian, the waiting was almost worse than the battle he'd already been fighting; every delay felt like time slipping through his fingers.

Eventually, their search led them to a small parish outside Glennisburg, Oklahoma. They couldn't find a number for either of them, so they decided to pack a few things and then head straight for Glennisburg.

They reach Glennisburg just after two in the morning. The town was quiet, the streets were empty,and exhaustion finally caught up with them.

They decided to stop at a local motel and rent a room for the rest of the night. In the motel, as they were starting to drift off to sleep, they talked about various things, ranging from Sebastian's service and why Charlotte decided to join the police force. To them, it was a welcome relief from the battle that Sebastian had been fighting for what felt like forever.

Morning came too soon. The motel room was still dim, the air heavy with stale quiet, and neither of them felt much like eating. They skipped breakfast without discussing it, moving through their routines with a shared sense of purpose.

The drive to the parish was short but silent. As the sun rose over Glennisburg, the small town began to stir, unaware of the weight pressing down on the car moving through its streets. Sebastian watched the church come into view, its modest structure standing calm and unassuming against the morning light. His chest tightened. If Father John was right, the men inside could finally put an end to what had been haunting him. If he was wrong... Sebastian didn't let himself finish the thought.

Charlotte pulled into the lot and cut the engine. For a moment, neither of them moved. Then she reached for the door, steady and certain, and Sebastian followed her inside, hoping this place held answers, and fearing what those answers might demand.

CHAPTER 15

When they arrived at the parish, they were amazed by how simple it looked. They had pictured a massive stone cathedral with sprawling gardens in their minds. Instead, it was just a modest wooden structure—a two-room building with a wooden cross mounted over the door. When they entered, the interior was equally unadorned: eight pews on either side and a small wooden altar on a raised platform. As they looked around, a priest approached and greeted them, asking what brought them there. Sebastian explained that they were looking for Father Carlos and Father Sean. The priest smiled. "I'm Father Carlos. Father Sean just stepped out to pick something up from the store, but I can help you if you don't want to wait." Sebastian decided not to wait. With Charlotte's help, he told the priest everything, filling in the details he couldn't quite remember. After they finished explaining—including how Father John had recommended the two priests to Sebastian—Father Carlos sat in silence for a few moments before speaking. Father Carlos looked at them both, his expression somber. "I'm deeply saddened to hear of Father John's passing. He was a good man, one who would give the shirt off his back if he knew it would help someone." He paused, choosing his words carefully. "I don't know if Father Sean and I can clear something that powerful on our own. We'd need considerable help and protection. But if we can bring in a third priest, I believe we could overcome this entity." He leaned forward. "I do hope we can clear this presence so we can reclaim Father John's body. It would help put him to rest." They continued talking until Father Sean returned. After they filled him in on everything they'd discussed, he agreed that they would need a third priest. The two priests then excused themselves, leaving Sebastian and Charlotte alone so they could discuss who would be the best fit to help them banish the entity. Alone in the church, Charlotte turned to Sebastian. "I'm not going to lie—I'm nervous about all this. I know I've never been in the house before, but I want to be there to see this through to the end. I've been here throughout this journey, making sure everything goes smoothly, but I want to be at the final confrontation to make sure we finish this right." She met his eyes. "Thank you for allowing me to help you with this final leg of the battle." Sebastian looked at her and pulled her into a hug. "Thank you for being there to keep me from giving up when I thought all hope was lost

CHAPTER 16

By the time the two priests returned, it was one in the afternoon, and both were smiling, giving Sebastian and Charlotte a glimmer of hope. Father Carlos was the first to speak. "We didn't just find one extra priest to help us — we found two. We also received help from Sister Mary Louise, who has been a nun for twenty-seven years and worked with Father John for twelve of them. The priest joining us is Father Hector. He's been a priest for sixty-two years, just one year shy of how long Father John served." Sebastian nodded when Father Carlos finished, then asked when everyone would be ready to leave for his house. Father Sean answered. "Father Hector and Sister Mary Louise should arrive tomorrow afternoon. After that, we'd need to gather our supplies and everything required to combat the entity, which would take the rest of that day. So I'd say we should be ready to leave for your house in two days' time — to cleanse it and retrieve Father John's body." Sebastian agreed, and he and Charlotte rose to leave for another night at the motel when Father Carlos stopped them, offering to let them stay at his place until they departed. At first, Sebastian and Charlotte were reluctant, not wanting to intrude on Father Carlos's privacy, but after some gentle insisting, they agreed.

When they arrived at Father Carlos's house, they gathered around the table while food was cooking and talked — about their lives, how they got to where they were, and what had brought them down the roads they now walked. At the end of the day, they settled in, Sebastian on the couch and Charlotte in the spare bedroom, and slowly drifted off to sleep, holding onto the hope that they would soon be free of this nightmare.